I FELT SAD
Bens life in quarantine

**Written and illustrated by
Fajsin Ali**

I FELT SAD

FIRST PAPERBACK EDITION MAY 2020

BOOK DESIGN AND ALL ILLUSTRATION BY FAJSIN ALI

ISBN 979 8 64225 044 0 (PAPERBACK)
PUBLISHED BY AMAZON KDP

@FAJSIN.ALI.POETRY

CRIMSONBOOKS620@GMAIL.COM

DEDICATED TO MY WONDERFUL
MOTHER & FATHER

Today I woke up feeling sad.
Things had changed.

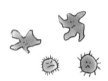

There was a new bug
and it was making people very sick.

We had to stay indoors
and only leave the house for
important things like medication and food.

I would sit and worry
about everyone I knew.

I missed my friends

I missed my teachers

The schools and shops
were closed.

I couldn't see my cousins
or even my grandparents.

One day, my mum,
my dad and I were eating breakfast.

There was a tingle in my nose
and my chin began to quiver.

All of a sudden, I began to cry.
I cried and I cried and I cried.

My parents hugged me tight.
They asked me what the problem was.

I told them how much
I missed my friends,
my family and how much
I missed playing in the park.

My parents sat and listened.
They told me this wasn't forever
and brighter days will come.

I felt a little bit better,
a little bit happy.

We sat together
and came up with all the things
we could do indoors
to keep happy.

We did some art,
story making,
cooking and baking.

I even got to face-time my relatives
and friends- that was fun!

I didn't feel sad anymore because
brighter days were coming!

The End

A BIG cheer for the
National Health Service (NHS)
and other frontline workers!

Hi adults!

If your little ones enjoyed
reading this book,
why not ask them to draw a
picture of all
the things they've been
getting up to during quarantine.

Feel free to post it
on Instagram and tag
@fajsin.ali.poetry

Printed by Amazon Italia Logistica S.r.l.
Torrazza Piemonte (TO), Italy

13584530R00016